AF668481

The Best Birthday Ever

Om KIDZ
An imprint of Om Books International

Om Kidz | Om Books International

Reprinted in 2023

Corporate & Editorial Office
A-12, Sector 64, Noida 201 301
Uttar Pradesh, India
Phone: +91 120 477 4100
Email: editorial@ombooks.com
Website: www.ombooksinternational.com

Sales Office
107, Ansari Road, Darya Ganj
New Delhi 110 002, India
Phone: +91 11 4000 9000
Email: sales@ombooks.com
Website: www.ombooks.com

© Om Books International 2017

ISBN: 978-93-52760-21-3

Printed in India

10 9 8 7 6 5 4 3 2

ALL RIGHTS RESERVED. No part of this book may be reproduced or transmitted in any form by any means, electronic or mechanical, including photocopying and recording, or by any information storage and retrieval system, except as may be expressly permitted in writing by the publisher.

The Best Birthday Ever

Paste your photograph here

My name is

____

Bob is a **bright boy**.
He jumps out of his **bed**
happily. It is his **birthday**!

Bob turns five today.

Bob is a **big boy** now!

He runs out of his **bedroom**.

Bob bounces down the stairs. He wants his Mom to wish him a happy **birthday**.

Bob's Mom is **baking** in the kitchen. She is wearing a **blue** shirt.

Bob hugs his Mom.
She kisses him and gives
him a **bowl** of cereal.

But Bob is not happy.
Bob's Mom did not wish
him a happy **birthday**!

TIMES TODAY

Bob's dad sits next to him.
He is wearing a **brown** shirt.
He too does not wish **Bob** a
happy **birthday**.

Bob goes **back** to his room. He feels very **bad**. He **begins** to pack his **bag**.

“**Both** my parents do not love me,” he thinks, “I will go to Granny’s house. She will come pick me up in a **bus**.”

Just then, **Bob** hears a **bell**.
Someone is at the door.
"Who could it **be**?"
wonders **Bob**.

Bob's friends are at the door with gifts! "Happy **Birthday**!" They yell together. **Bob**'s Mom and dad have thrown him a surprise party!

Bob's Mom has **baked** a **birthday** cake for him.

Bob’s dad gifts him a **beautiful bike**.

Bob is surprised. He is also very happy. This has **been** the **best birthday** ever!

Know your words

Naming words

Bob	bedroom	bag
boy	bowl	bus
bed	bell	
birthday	bike	

Describing words

bright	brown	bad
big	beautiful	back
blue	best	

Doing words

baking bounces

Sight words

both	be	been
begin		

Colour the gifts with words starting with the letter '**Bb**'.

What did Bob's Mom bake for him?
Join the dots to find out.
Don't forget to colour too.

Match the following words beginning with the letter '**Bb**' with their images.

bus • • 

bike • • 

bed • • 

bag • • 

bowl • •